by Charles Carney

illustrated by Seonna Hong

Stephen Hillenburg

Based on the TV series SpongeBob SquarePants™ created by

Stephen Hillenburg.

Cover and internal design by Susan Choi

Published by Sourcebooks Jabberwocky, an imprint of Sourcebooks, Inc.
P.O. Box 4410, Naperville, Illinois 60567-4410
(630) 961-3900
Fax: (630) 961-2168
www.jabberwockykids.com

Library of Congress Cataloging-in-Publication data is on file with the publisher.

Source of Production: Leo Paper, Heshan City, Guangdong Province, China
Date of Production: September 2014
Run Number: 5002193
Printed and bound in China.

LEO 10 9 8 7 6 5 4 3 2 1

Goodnight, goodnight SpongeBob SquarePants

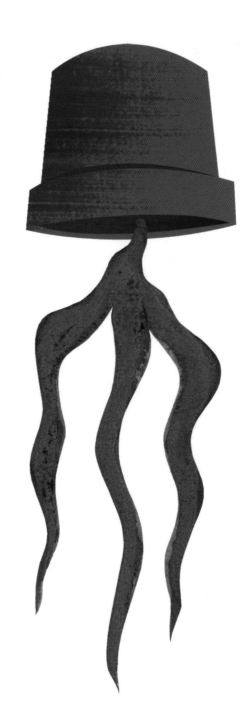

Goodnight plants

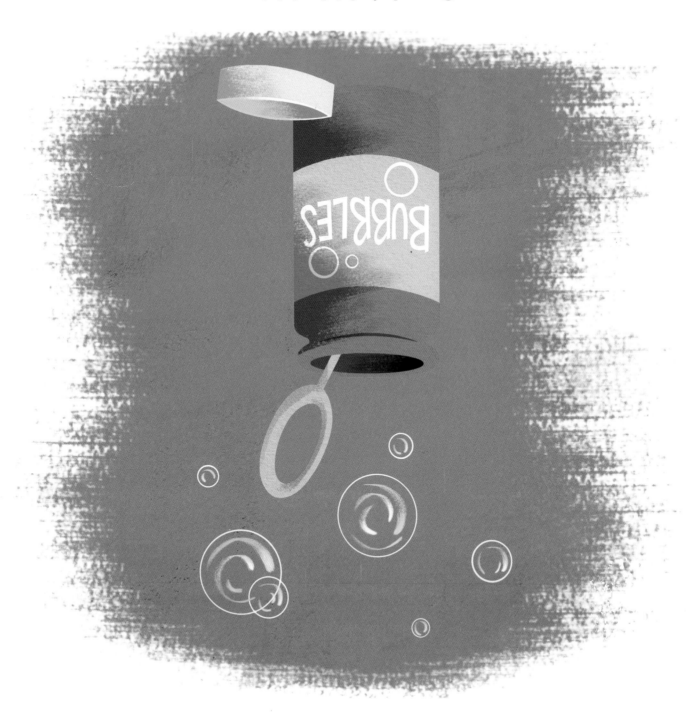

Goodnight bubbles

And goodnight Patrick
(who's still asleep)

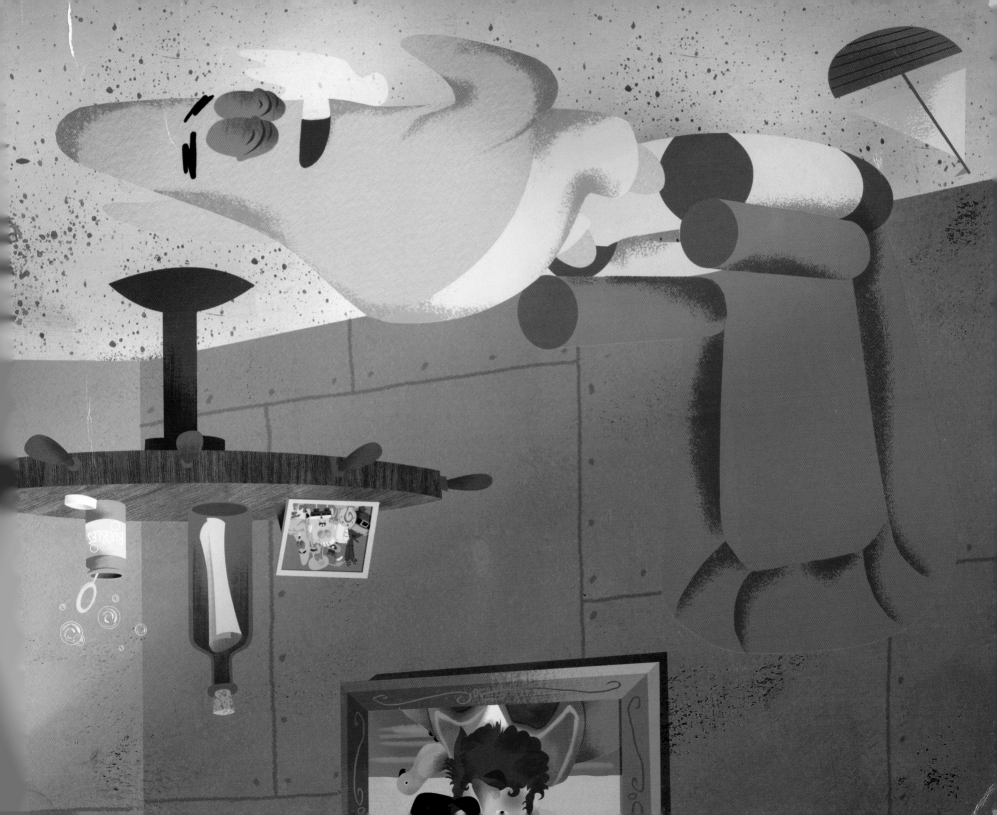

Goodnight nighttime crawler

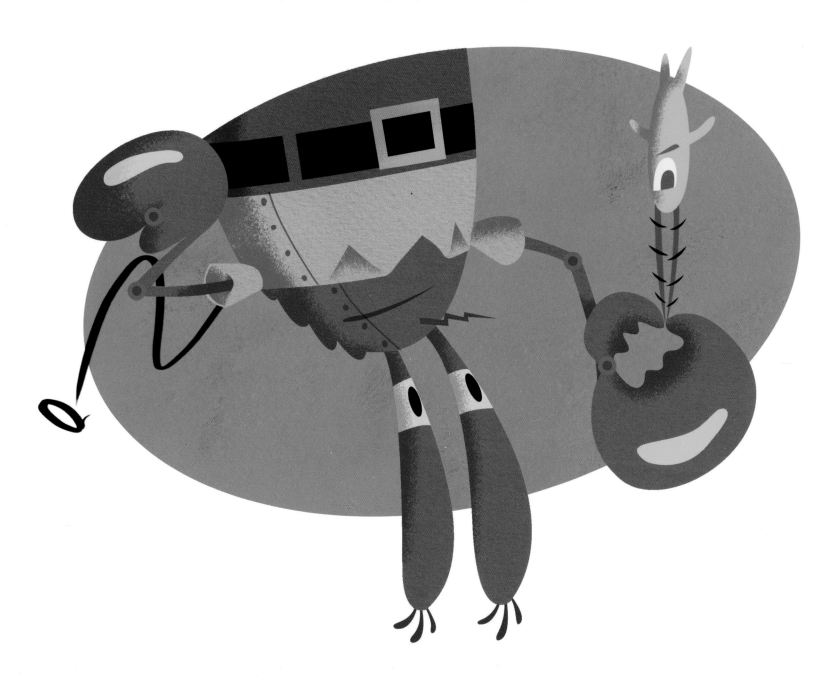

Goodnight friends

Goodnight boss with dollars

Goodnight squirrel that hollers

Goodnight meowing snail!

Goodnight boat with a sail

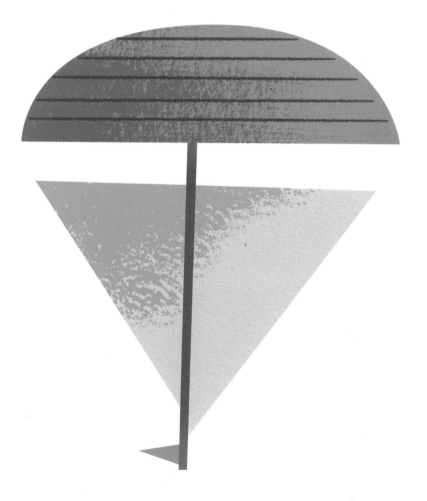

And goodnight Krabby Patty mixture

Goodnight pirate picture

And goodnight Patrick
(who's already asleep)

Goodnight fishes of the deep

Goodnight diving board
Goodnight foghorn

Goodnight net
And the hero balloons

Goodnight octopus with a face like a prune

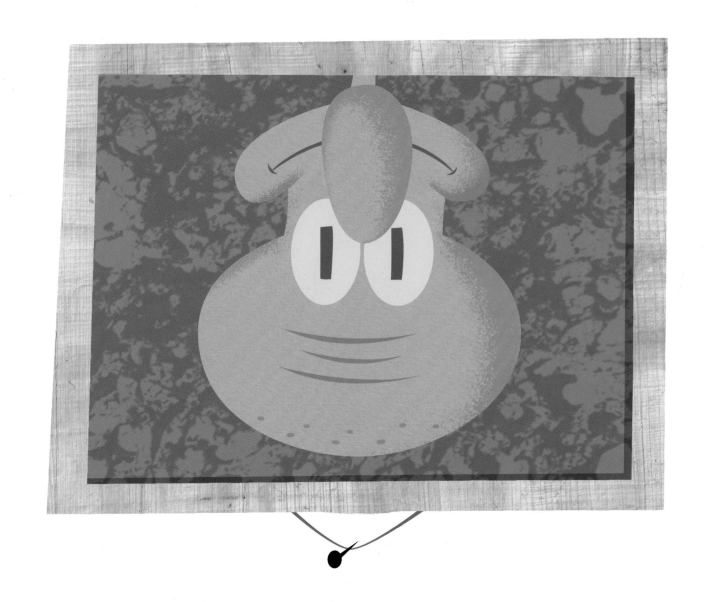

Goodnight room

And Plankton,
the nighttime crawler

And a squirrel that hollers
And a boss with dollars

And a long jellyfishing net
And a meowing snail for a pet

And a high-dive board
And a clock-foghorn

And there were three mattresses
to make one bed

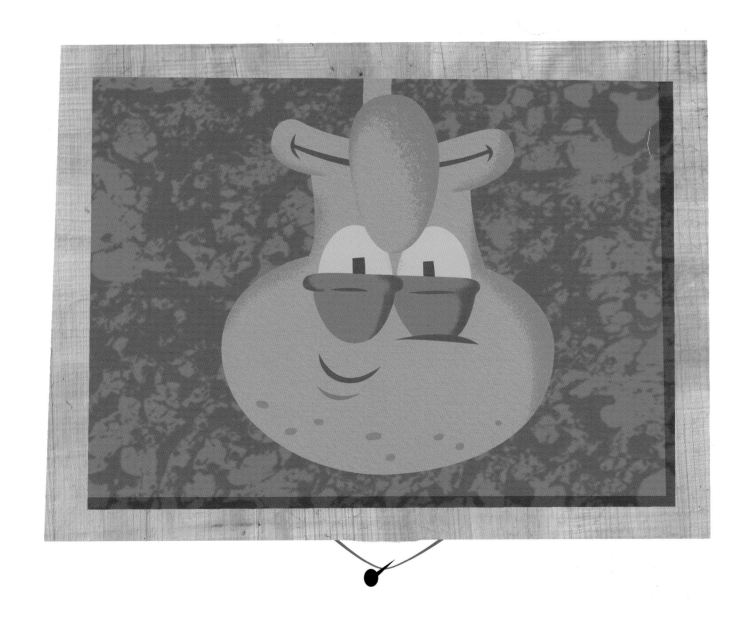

In the pineapple room
There was a sponge in pajamas
And superhero balloons
And a picture of...

SpongeBob SquarePants

Goodnight Lagoon

A parody from
Bikini Bottom

By Charles Carney

Illustrated by
Seonna Hong